CARNIVAL

Julie Sykes

Illustrated by Martin Salisbury

OXFORD
UNIVERSITY PRESS

OXFORD
UNIVERSITY PRESS

Great Clarendon Street, Oxford OX2 6DP

Oxford University Press is a department of the University of Oxford.
It furthers the University's objective of excellence in research, scholarship,
and education by publishing worldwide in

Oxford   New York

Auckland   Cape Town   Dar es Salaam   Hong Kong   Karachi
Kuala Lumpur   Madrid   Melbourne   Mexico City   Nairobi
New Delhi   Shanghai   Taipei   Toronto

With offices in

Argentina   Austria   Brazil   Chile   Czech Republic   France   Greece
Guatemala   Hungary   Italy   Japan   Poland   Portugal   Singapore
South Korea   Switzerland   Thailand   Turkey   Ukraine   Vietnam

Oxford is a registered trade mark of Oxford University Press
in the UK and in certain other countries

British Library Cataloguing in Publication Data
Data available

ISBN-13: 978-0-19-918452-1
ISBN-10: 0-19-918452-6

1 3 5 7 9 10 8 6 4 2

Available in packs
Stage 16 Pack of 6:
ISBN-13: 978-0-19-918456-9; ISBN-10: 0-19-918456-9
Stage 16 Class Pack:
ISBN-13: 978-0-19-918453-8; ISBN-10: 0-19-918453-4
Guided Reading Cards also available:
ISBN-13: 978-0-19-918455-2; ISBN-10: 0-19-918455-0

Cover artwork by Annabel Hartmann

Printed in Great Britain by
Ashford Colour Press, Gosport Hants

For Linda Jennings

CHAPTER 1

The ambulance

The sound of an engine woke Clare. Unusual.
Living in a close there was no through traffic. No
traffic at all. Old Max Parry next door didn't
have a car. Neither did Mrs Angel the other side.
Clare lay in the darkness, alert, until a light
began flashing; its beam dancing through the
curtain, sending shadows across the ceiling.

At once she was out of bed and pulling back
the curtain. In the road below an ambulance
drew up, its blue light silently flashing. Clare
grabbed the dressing gown from the end of her
bed, crammed her feet into slippers and ran

downstairs. The front door was bolted and she needed a chair to reach the top one. With trembling fingers she forced back the lock nearly losing her balance in haste. She dropped the chair in the hall and shot through the door running towards the ambulance at full pelt.

'Whoa there, stand back, little lady.'

A hand caught her wrist stopping her before she reached the vehicle's open doors.

'Max,' she croaked wriggling herself free. 'Where is he?'

'Coming out now, stand back,' said the ambulance driver.

Clare ignored her, running across the garden towards the stretcher coming out from the front door.

'Max.'

His face was pale against the red blanket covering him. He looked old and frail yet terribly young all at the same time.

'Max.' Clare's voice was little more than a whisper as she leant forward and touched his cheek.

Slowly he opened his eyes. The blanket

moved as if he was trying to take hold of her hand.

'Clare.'

She put her ear close to his lips to hear what he was saying.

'Clare . . . good girl. Don't worry . . . Look after Carnival.'

His face contorted with pain and Clare stroked his head.

'Something for you. Something to remind you . . .' Max gasped and made one last effort. 'Something for you on Carnival. Special. You'll know what. Something to remind you of us. Me and Carnival. Meant to write it down. Too late now. Make sure you find it.'

'Stand back please.'

A hand on her shoulder guided Clare from the stretcher and she was surprised to see she was standing back by the ambulance doors. Carefully the crew lifted Max inside and the last thing she saw was an oxygen mask being fastened against his face.

Doors slammed, voices murmured and a light came towards her. It was Mum carrying a torch.

'Clare! What are you doing? You'll catch your death.'

At her mother's choice of words Clare felt tears, hot and salty, roll down her cheeks.

'Come back inside. Come on. It'll be all right. You'll see.'

She let her mother lead her back indoors into the lounge where she reluctantly drank a cup of cocoa made for her by Alan. He'd stayed the night then. Clare knew he would and hated herself for minding when Max needed her thoughts more. And when, early next morning, Mrs Francis phoned the hospital Clare hated herself again. Max was dead. From a massive heart attack in the ambulance. She'd been bothered about Alan staying the night when all the while Max was dead. He hadn't even made it to hospital.

CHAPTER 2

Carnival

Clare refused to talk about it. Every time Mum mentioned Max she changed the subject. Mum had said it would be all right but it wasn't. She shouldn't have said that. Clare held onto her grief till her insides felt like a shaken bottle of lemonade. She couldn't believe that Max had gone, couldn't believe she'd never see him again. She kept remembering things to tell him then remembering that she couldn't. It was awful.

The funeral was arranged for the following Tuesday. Four days after the start of the Easter holiday and exactly one week after Max had died. It caused a row. For the first time after his death Clare found herself speaking of Max. She started by telling Mum about the promise he'd made. The last words he'd spoken to her. Mum scoffed but gently.

'Old people say things they don't mean. They get confused.'

'Max wasn't confused,' said Clare stubbornly. 'He knew what he was saying.'

'Maybe Max *did* want you to have something to remember him and that old cruiser by.' Mrs Francis ran a hand through her curls in a helpless gesture. 'But unless he wrote it down no one will believe you. There'll be plenty of relatives queuing up for their share of his things, you'll see.'

'Carnival's a narrow boat not a cruiser.'

Clare fought back tears.

'If Max said that he'd left me something special then he did. I want to go and look.'

'When? Carnival doesn't belong to Max any more. You'll have to get permission from the new owner. Whoever that is!'

'I'm going after the funeral. It won't take long. The new owner needn't know.'

Mrs Francis put her arm around Clare's shoulders and made her sit on the sofa.

'About the funeral. We, I . . . I don't think you should go.'

'What do you mean *we?*'

Clare rounded on her mother, her hazel eyes hot with anger.

'You mean Alan says I can't go?'

'Alan agrees with me. A funeral is no place for a child of your age,' said Mrs Francis. 'You can send flowers instead. I'll give you the money.'

Clare hated Alan. With his pale blue eyes and his receding hairline and the way his stomach hung over the top of his trousers. But most of all she hated the way he interfered with her life. Sticking his nose in where it wasn't wanted. She wanted to hate her mother too. But Mum was all she had now. Dad left when Clare was a baby and had a new family; a younger wife and two little boys. They sent Christmas cards and a cheque on her birthday but they never invited her to stay. Clare took the flower money and put it in a collection box for the disabled children. Max would have been pleased. He liked children.

On the morning of the funeral she watched the hearse arrive from her bedroom window, crawling along like a big, black beetle. She didn't wait to see it leave. Taking her bicycle from the shed she cycled quickly away. Forbidden to go to the funeral she cycled all morning and finally she went down to the canal. To Carnival.

The old boat sat in the water like a floating rose garden, a riot of colour on a blue background.

'Carnival, Loxford.'

Clare spoke the words like she was talking to a friend.

Carnival hadn't always come from Loxford. Max bought her in Liverpool when she was little more than a shell and brought her home to restore her. It kept him busy in the early days of retirement and when she was finished he renamed her Carnival.

Clare parked her bicycle in the usual spot a few feet from the towpath and boarded the boat. Around her neck, like a good luck charm, hung a small key. She pulled it over her head and fitted it into the galley doors pushing them open. Then for a moment she was unable to move as the air inside rushed up to meet her. Max. The smell was overpowering. It was as if he were there, in another room, and any minute would call out, 'Come in, come in. There's apple juice in the fridge.'

Clare didn't want to remember. It hurt. She propped open the doors then turned to the windows, pushing them wide, welcoming new air inside. Clare knew that Max had left her something special. She would find it and go home. Quickly she began to search.

Max was a tidy person. He hated clutter. Clare found nothing in the galley, or the dining area. She skipped the tiny bathroom, stopping outside the cabin. Max's room. It was fitted with bunk beds so he could sleep over, which he did in the summer.

'What am I looking for? Is it in here?'

She opened the door and stepped inside. She stood in the gloom clenching her teeth and fists to stop the tears stinging her eyes. She opened the blind, concentrated on the sun filling the room with light. She started with the tiny wardrobe facing the bunks, closing it hurriedly when she saw the coat hanger with his old work trousers on.

'What did you want me to have?'

The cupboard, full of cloths and towels, smelt of fabric conditioner. But under the bunks was a box. A large

wooden box with Max's initials painted in black. It was locked. She lay down and reached towards it, her fingers touching its varnished surface. Was this it? Was the something special locked away in here?

Suddenly the floor rocked. Someone was coming aboard. Clare scrambled to her feet and looked around. Where could she hide? She wouldn't fit under the bed. What about the wardrobe? Carnival was still rocking on the water as she put one foot inside. She felt a draught as the cabin door opened but wasn't quick enough. Before she could disappear from sight someone grabbed her arms. A voice, not the person holding her but someone else, said, 'Who's that then?'

CHAPTER 3

The decision

Clare looked down, letting her hair cover her face like a brown curtain. She didn't want her captors, two boys, one much older than the other, to know how close to tears she was. It would have been easier if they were cross with her but they weren't. They were sympathetic and kind.

'David Parry and my brother, Martin,' said the older boy, stiffly offering his hand for Clare to shake. 'We've come from the funeral. Max was our great uncle.'

'Are you Clare?' asked Martin shyly. 'Mrs

Angel told us to look out for you.'

'I bet she did,' thought Clare sourly. Mrs Angel was Max's other neighbour and a right old busybody.

Martin looked roughly the same age as Clare, slightly built like herself, and his brown hair stuck up in a tuft at the top.

'Thanks for looking after Carnival. It's mine now. Max left it to me.'

Clare stayed silent.

'I still can't believe it's mine. Even though we're taking it home tomorrow.'

'She,' said Clare. 'A boat's a she not an it.'

Martin laughed apologetically.

'I don't know anything about boats. I didn't know Max very well either. I'd love to know why he gave me Carnival.'

'Where's home?' interrupted Clare.

'Merton, on the River Wavel. Mum and Dad have rented moorings there close to our house.'

'Merton,' said Clare slowly. An idea was forming in her mind. 'That's a long way. Lots of locks. Can your mum and dad work a lock?'

Martin chuckled and David raised an eyebrow.

'Mum and Dad aren't coming with us. They hate water! I'm looking after Martin.'

Clare felt a spark of excitement. No parents on their homeward trip! It made her plan even simpler. Casually she asked, 'Can you work a lock then?'

David waved his hand airily and Clare thought he looked like an actor, especially with his dark, curly hair and bright blue eyes.

'Nope, but I've got a book that tells you everything there is to know about canals.'

'Can you work a lock?' asked Martin.

'Yes, I can. I sailed with Max all the time. I know all the locks on this canal and I know how to sail Carnival.'

'You must have known Max really well. What was he like? We only met him twice.'

'He was . . .'

Suddenly words failed Clare. Max was everything to her and now nothing. An icy hand gripped her insides and with tears stinging her eyes she elbowed her way past the boys and ran into the corridor. She shouldn't be here. Carnival was no longer her special place. She had come to say a private farewell and to collect the keepsake that Max had left her. Martin and David had ruined that so now she must leave.

In the dining area Clare stopped running and sat on the long bench. She couldn't give up yet. Surely she owed more to Max. He wanted her to have something from him. Something more than the few snapshots and memories she already had. Silently she waited and after a bit Martin and David joined her sitting across the table from her. David offered her a crumpled tissue and gratefully Clare took it and blew her nose.

She peered at the boys from under her fringe.

'Boating isn't as easy as it looks. Narrow boats have a mind of their own. Then there's all the rules of the road and that sort of thing. Do you know enough about it to take Carnival home tomorrow?'

'We have to,' said Martin. 'We're going on holiday next week and the week after that we go back to school and college. David's got exams.'

Clare took a steadying breath. She needed it for what she was about to say next. Never, in her whole life, had she been so forward.

'I could come with you. I know Carnival and I know the canal.'

She dug her nails in her palms and stared at the table so she didn't have to look at Martin. She wouldn't blush. This was no time to be squeamish. She owed this to Max.

'Come with us? What, all the way to Merton?'

'If you want.'

'I don't know. We don't know you. We might not like each other.'

Martin sounded confused.

'Thanks,' said David kindly. 'But there isn't enough room. There's only one bedroom.'

'This is a bedroom too.'

Clare patted the bench she was sitting on.

'This unfolds into a bed. Let me come with you. I'd be a big help. I'm not bossy or anything.'

Martin turned to face David.

'Uncle Max would have let her wouldn't he?'

'I dunno,' answered David. 'But it's not up to him. It's up to me. I'm in charge until we get home. It's a big enough responsibility without taking on an extra one.'

'It would be better if I had someone of my own age to talk to. You said you had heaps of revision to do.'

'I dunno, Martin. It's a big responsibility.'

David drummed his fingers on the small dining table.

'All right,' he said at length. 'If Mum and Dad don't mind and Clare's parents agree. And on the condition that you both behave yourselves. I'll phone Mum and Dad tonight. There's a phone box in the village.'

Clare's face burnt with embarrassment.

'Thanks,' she whispered. She was too breathless to say anything else.

Pedalling home at breakneck speed Clare rehearsed a speech for her mother. The Parrys, Max's nephews, needed her. They didn't know anything about boats. She was doing them a big favour.

'They need me, they need me, they need me.'

She pedalled faster singing the words out loud until she began to believe them. How good they sounded. No one needed her these days. Mum had once but not now, not since she'd met Alan. Despite the wind, chilly for April, Clare felt warm inside. Warmed by the thought of being needed, her heart swelled like a balloon.

In the front garden Clare dropped her bike and tore indoors. The television was on in the lounge and she headed towards it.

'Mum?'

She opened the lounge door and the balloon in her heart burst.

Alan was sprawled on the sofa, watching the television.

'Hi, had a good bike ride?'

Clare looked at the floor so she couldn't see the top of his balding head. Why was Mum going out with such a creep? She could have chosen anyone she wanted. Mum was pretty, everyone said so. She had lovely hair, and her curls were real not permed.

'Mum?' she called again and when her mother's voice answered from the kitchen Clare closed the lounge door and hurried towards it.

'Hello, love. It's spaghetti bolognaise for tea. Your favourite.'

'Is he staying?' asked Clare stiffly.

'Yes, dear. Alan is staying. He's offered to take you down to the video shop later to get that film you wanted.'

'I don't want a video and I don't want any tea either,' said Clare rudely.

She pushed her mother out of the way and ran up to her room. She'd hurt Mum but so what? Mum knew that Clare hated Alan and she'd just have to choose. Alan or her. It couldn't be both.

Clare lay on the bed and stared at the ceiling. There was no point in asking Mum about Carnival tonight. Alan would say no. He always did. Then an alarming thought struck her. What if Alan stayed the night? He often did. David said they were leaving really early in the morning so there wouldn't be time to ask Mum before Alan went to work.

'I've got to go with Carnival tomorrow.'

It was Clare's only chance of finding the gift Max had left her. After that, Carnival would be gone, like Max. The more she thought about it, the more Clare knew there was only one solution. It was her life. She wouldn't ask. She would just go.

CHAPTER 4

Looking for the key

Carnival was still there and Clare stood for a
moment admiring her. The glossy blue
paintwork was decorated with the traditional
roses and castle design. On top of the roof, in
earthenware pots, were masses of flowers; all
chosen and planted by Max. Don't think of Max.
Think of something else, quickly. Clare pushed
her fringe out of her eyes and hurried towards
Carnival.

'Hi.' Martin opened the galley doors and
hailed her. 'You're just in time for breakfast.'

A delicious smell of fried bacon drifted from

the galley and Clare's stomach groaned. She thought of the money stuffed at the bottom of her rucksack. She'd packed sparingly and there had been no chance to raid the kitchen for food. But she wasn't a scrounger. She could pay her way. Luckily she had money saved in her money box and a cheque sent by Dad for Easter instead of an Easter egg. Clare had left the cheque in her mother's purse and removed the same amount of cash. She wasn't a scrounger and she wasn't a thief either.

'Is there enough for me?'

'There's heaps.'

Martin held out his hand to help Clare aboard.

Clare smiled.

'Thanks,' she said, hopping lightly onto the deck and Martin nodded.

In the galley David stood over the tiny hob, a fish slice in his hand.

'Where's your mother? I thought she'd come down to meet me.'

Clare had thought of this already. Her mother would never let her go off with someone she didn't know. When Max first offered her a trip on Carnival he invited Mrs Francis too. And she had gone with them, not just once but many times until they knew Max properly, even though he was a neighbour!

'Mum's on an early shift this week,' said Clare. 'She asked Mrs Angel about you. The neighbour at the funeral. Mrs Angel said that you seemed responsible enough. Mum gave me a note for you.'

Clare had typed the note herself, on Mum's old typewriter. She'd got the idea from Stacy Watts, a girl at school. She played truant for three whole weeks before anyone caught on to her. She kept writing herself sick notes on her dad's computer. David took a long time reading the note and Clare hoped he couldn't tell how hard her heart was thudding against her chest.

'I suppose this is all right,' he said at last. 'My parents know you're coming with us but Mum wants to speak to your mum. I said I'd ring her tonight and give her your mother's phone number.'

'No problem,' said Clare.

She thrust her hands inside her pockets so David wouldn't notice how they were trembling. Tonight was a lifetime away. Hopefully she would have found what she was looking for by then and it wouldn't matter anyway.

'Great!' said Martin. 'Is breakfast ready? I'm starving.'

'You're always starving,' replied David. 'Have you had breakfast yet, Clare?'

Clare shook her head.

'Bacon? Two rashers or three?'

'Two please.'

Clare stood awkwardly while David prodded the bacon.

'You can sit down,' said Martin.

'Get her to make the tea,' said David. He grinned cheekily. 'She might as well start earning her keep.'

Pleased to have something useful to do Clare busied herself filling the kettle and setting out mugs.

'David boiled it over last night,' said Martin conversationally. 'He made a right mess. We're not used to gas. Our kettle's electric at home and it switches itself off.'

'What have you done with the tea?'

In her hands Clare held open Max's tea caddy, a green tin with a picture of a moorhen on one side. The tin was full of boiled sweets.

'It's in the jar, the blue one.'

'The sugar jar,' thought Clare but she put the tea bags into the mugs without comment.

Breakfast was a hurried affair and Clare was glad. She was eager to leave in case Mum and Alan woke early and discovered she was missing. It would be just like Alan to come looking for her and force her to go back home. She felt a rush of relief when David got up and carelessly piled the dirty dishes into the sink.

'We'll wash up later,' he announced. 'It's time we were off.'

Martin and David had taken Carnival on a short trip the day before and they started the engine and cast off without any trouble. Clare untied the rope securing the bow while Martin released the stern. David took the tiller to steer the boat.

There was friendly teasing between Martin and David when Martin asked for a turn at the helm.

'Sure, if you can find a box.'

'Ha, ha,' said Martin. He pulled a face at David and said to Clare, 'He thinks I'm not big enough to see over the top of the cabin roof!'

'I can see over it and you're taller than me,' said Clare earnestly.

'Two shrimps,' exclaimed David. 'Alone on a boat with two of them!'

'We didn't ask you to come with us, did we?'

Martin looked to Clare for support.

'No, but Mum and Dad would never have agreed to you going off on your own. Besides, I couldn't let my only brother drown, could I?'

'Huh! I can swim better than you! And I bet my driving's better if you'd just let me have a go.'

'Driving!' mocked David. 'You don't drive a boat, you sail it. Isn't that right, Clare?'

Clare nodded and grinned at Martin to let him know she wasn't taking sides.

'Brothers, who'd have 'em?' asked Martin. 'Have you got any brothers or sisters?'

'No,' said Clare. Half brothers didn't count, especially as she'd never met hers.

'Lucky you. I wish I was an only child.'

'It's lonely sometimes.'

Clare spoke the words without thinking. There was something about Martin that made it easy to tell him things she'd never mentioned before.

'You should get a pet. A dog or something.'

Clare had never thought about having a pet. She didn't have much to do with animals. Perhaps a pet would be nice. But then there was Alan.

'Alan wouldn't let me have one.'

'Who's Alan?'

'Mum's boyfriend. He doesn't like me.'

There was an awkward silence then Martin said, 'Can I have a turn at steering?'

'Sure,' said David. 'Nice and easy remember. She's a canal barge not a speed boat.'

Martin was good. He held the tiller lightly and concentrated on the canal. His green eyes had the same calm expression that Max had when sailing and this pleased Clare.

Carnival would be in safe hands with Martin. She leaned against the rail and relaxed. It was going to be all right. She might even tell Martin about Max's promise. Perhaps he had the key to the mystery box hidden under Max's bed. For Clare was sure that's where Max had hidden the keepsake he wanted her to have.

As they approached Ryden's Lock David suggested they moored up for a bit.

'We've made good time. I'm thirsty. Let's stop for a drink.'

'I'll make the drinks,' Clare offered, eager to please.

'Well be careful then. The kettle spits if you overfill it. I don't want you scalding yourself.'

Clare knew the kettle spat but she didn't say anything.

'I'll have coke,' said Martin. 'I'll get it.'

'It's all right. I'll do it.'

While the kettle was boiling Clare pulled two cans of cola from the tiny fridge. Someone had moved the glasses and as she searched for them a thought came to her. People often left keys in their kitchen. What if Martin did have the key to the wooden box and he'd put it in the galley for safe keeping? Idly she opened a drawer and began to riffle through it. Most of the things she recognized as belonging to Max but there were a few new things. Like the pair of designer sunglasses, an address book and a long tin with a picture of Mickey Mouse on the lid. The tin rattled when she moved it. Clare picked it up and held it for a moment. It was cold and smooth. Mickey Mouse grinned up at her.

'Open me,' he invited.

The kettle began to boil. Clare didn't notice as she prised open the tin.

'What are you doing?'

David's voice was cold as a Siberian wind.

'I . . .'

Clare spun around. Her cheeks flamed as she stared at the wad of money spilling from her hands.

'I was . . .'

'You were what?'

'What's going on?'

Martin appeared at the galley doors and rescued the kettle from the hob.

'Where's my coke?'

'Forget the coke,' said David. 'I've caught a thief.'

CHAPTER 5

David and Martin

It was awful. Standing there with the tin open, feeling as if the metal was burning a hole straight through her hands. She looked at the money, unable to meet David's eyes.

'It's not what you think. I'm not a thief. I was looking for some matches.' Clare's voice rose and her words came faster as she defended herself. 'We're nearly out. Max kept a spare box in a tin, to stop them from getting damp.'

When neither of the boys answered, Clare thrust the money tin at David and picked up her rucksack from where she'd left it in the corner of the saloon.

'I'm not a thief.'

She rummaged in the bag, burrowing deeper and deeper until finally she found her purse.

'I brought money with me. See! I can pay my way.'

Martin's cheeks turned pink.

'Sorry, Clare,' he said quickly. 'Our mistake.'

'How do you know?' snapped David. 'You don't know her. You're too trusting, Martin.'

'Max trusted her. That neighbour said they were friends.'

David ran both hands through his hair stretching the thick, brown curls like elastic bands and letting them ping back into place.

'And he gave her a key,' Martin added.

'True. So I made a mistake. Sorry, Clare. Forget what I said.'

'Thanks.'

Clare dropped her head, not quite able to meet David in the eye. She wasn't a thief but she hadn't told the truth either.

'Matches,' said Martin, a little too brightly. 'We didn't think of those. Where can we get some?'

'Steep. It's a couple of miles from here. You go through Ryden's Lock and moor up at The Barley Mow pub. Then it's a half-hour walk. I've done it loads of times with Max.'

'Right,' said David briskly. 'That's what we'll do. Martin, you take the tiller. Clare, you can work the lock with me.'

On the way into town Clare found herself walking alongside Martin while David strode ahead. David was wearing his personal stereo and soon Clare and Martin found themselves talking like old friends. They were in the same year at school, first year of secondary and they liked the same things.

'Music,' said Clare. 'Except Alan makes me turn it down.'

'You don't like Alan do you?'

'He's not good enough for Mum. She's pretty, everyone says so. Her hair curls and she has lovely green eyes. Alan's got a beer belly and he's bald on top. It's gross.'

'Looks aren't everything, personality counts.'

'Alan hasn't got that either. He's bossy. He's always telling Mum what I should and shouldn't do. He doesn't like me having fun.'

'Have you told your mum about it?'

'No.'

'You should. Or maybe your real dad. What's he like?'

A muscle in Clare's cheek twitched and a shuttered look crossed her eyes.

'Don't see much of him. He lives too far away.'

'Bad luck. My dad's nice, you'd like him. Mum says he's a nut case. Says he leads us on.'

'Mum was good fun before Alan. She played her CDs really loud and we'd dance until our neighbour banged on the wall. Not Max of course. His house wasn't joined to ours.'

They continued in silence and suddenly Clare wanted to tell Martin about Max; how kind he was and how he made her laugh. Before she could begin though David stopped to wait for them. Clare clammed up immediately. She would wait and tell Martin about Max another time.

The town was busy with Easter shoppers and they queued for ages in the supermarket. David refused Clare's offer of money to pay for the matches and the extras they needed now there were three of them to feed.

'Is there an electrical shop nearby?' asked David, once they had finished. 'I need a new foil for my razor.'

'About time too,' teased Martin. 'Mum will have a fit if you go home with all that stubble. You look like a hedgehog!'

Clare giggled as she led the way to Tandom's, the largest electrical store in town. She'd never thought about having a brother or sister before but it was fun being with David and Martin. Perhaps things would be better at home if she had a brother or a sister. They could gang up on Alan and laugh about him!

Tandom's was busy too. Clare wandered over to the rows of televisions and watched the bank of silent screens all showing the same picture. The adverts finished and Clare recognized the start of the local news programme. She glanced at her watch in surprise and saw that it was almost tea-time. Mum would be dishing up the evening meal now, or would she? With a shock Clare realized her mother had no one to cook for but herself.

Then, to her horror, a face she knew appeared on the screen. It remained for a few seconds and Clare felt her eyes drawn across every television set in the shop.

Her scalp prickled, the backs of her hands began to itch and a sick feeling rose in the pit of her stomach. The camera panned back to the newsreader, his face sombre as he read his script. Even without any sound Clare knew what he was saying. The newsreader shuffled his papers ready for the next story.

The picture changed to a field of newly born lambs. Clare felt a tap on her shoulder.

'Ready? What's up? You look like you've seen a ghost.'

Clare took a grip of herself.

'I didn't realize how late it was. The shops will be closing soon. Has David got everything?'

She followed Martin out of the shop back into the crowded street. No, she hadn't seen a ghost she thought. It was her own picture that had shocked her. Last year's school photograph flashed across every screen on every television set in the shop. Before she could stop herself, Clare turned to see if anyone had followed her out into the street.

CHAPTER 6

The break-in

They didn't talk much on the way back. Clare kept her head down so that her dark hair covered her face in a sleek curtain. She was in shock. In her eagerness to find the gift from Max she'd put all thoughts of anyone else straight out of her head.

How stupid to go off without leaving a note for Mum. She never went anywhere without saying where she was going and when she'd be back. Poor Mum would be crazy with worry by now. But what could she do about it? She hadn't told Martin and David the truth. If she confessed now she'd have to explain why she'd run away. David had called her a thief. What would he say if he knew she hadn't told the truth either? He wouldn't believe her about Max's promise. And what would Martin think?

She liked Martin. They were getting on really well. Would he still be her friend if he knew how she'd lied?

'What's up?'

Clare started and David laughed.

'You were miles away.'

'I . . . oh, it was nothing,' mumbled Clare.

David gave Clare a curious look that left her feeling uncomfortable. Guilty conscience, she decided crossly, though she was sure that he hadn't seen her picture in the shop.

'I thought we'd stay where we are for the night. There's no rush now we've an experienced crewmember on board.' He smiled kindly at Clare and went on. 'I've got to phone Mum to give her your mother's telephone number. There must be a phone at that pub, the Barley Mow. I'll phone from there. You'll be all right on your own for a bit won't you?'

''Course we will,' said Martin.

'Sure?'

'Yeah, it'll be good fun.'

'Clare?'

If she was going to tell them the truth, now was her chance.

'Fine by me.'

Coward, she told herself miserably. Now she was going to have to tell more lies and the next one would be over her phone number. Clare already knew what she would do about that. She would give David the wrong number. She could always blame it on her untidy handwriting.

'That's settled then,' said David, looking pleased.

Back on board David cooked an enormous tea of sausages, mashed potatoes and baked beans. Martin laid the table and Clare made steaming mugs of tea.

'I'm starving,' said David.

He set the plates on the table placing a dish of extra sausages in the middle.

'Eat up, before it goes cold.'

It was a happy meal and Clare did her best to

join in the fun but her smile was forced and her stomach felt like it was lined with lead. She ate slowly, chewing each mouthful thoroughly, but still the food tasted like cardboard. It was a relief when the meal was over and David disappeared into his cabin to get ready to go out.

'What shall we do?' asked Martin. 'We could play Monopoly or Jenga?'

'Monopoly.'

Clare didn't think her hands would be steady enough for Jenga.

Before he left for the Barley Mow David lit the gas lamps in the saloon for them.

'I won't be late. Come and get me if there's a problem.'

'You sound like Mum,' said Martin, grinning.

David threw a cushion at him.

'Right then. I'm off. Behave yourselves!'

He left through the galley, closing the doors behind him, making the boat rock as he stepped onto the tow-path. Clare and Martin looked at each other shyly then Martin busied himself collecting the Monopoly set from his cabin and setting up the pieces.

'Who do you want to be?'

'The boat.'

Martin chose the car and picked up the money.

'Do you want to be banker?'

'No, you do it.'

They started playing and although Clare tried to enjoy the game, her heart wasn't really in it. When she'd decided to go with Carnival she thought she was taking control of her life. Now, she wasn't so sure. Things were moving too fast and she felt like she was free-wheeling down a steep hill. She could put on the brakes at any time but what then? Sometimes when you went too fast, braking was dangerous. You skidded and fell off and hurt yourself. Is that what would happen now if she put the brakes on and came clean with everyone?

'Have you slept on Carnival before?'

With a start Clare realized it was the second time Martin had asked the question.

'No, never. Max often did in the summer time. He liked to get up early in the morning to watch the birds.'

She looked around the cabin, noticing how the light outside was failing and the gas lamps were beginning to cast tiny, flickering shadows on the walls. It was warm and cosy and when Martin drew the curtains she felt safe and protected.

'Say when you want to go to bed.'

'It's a bit early yet,' Clare replied, yawning in spite of herself. 'But I am tired.'

At half past nine Martin helped Clare pull the bench out into a bed and fetched her a pillow and blankets. Before he went to his own cabin he said, 'I'm glad you came. It makes me feel a bit closer to Max. It's funny being left such a wonderful present by someone you hardly knew.'

As Clare washed her face and cleaned her teeth she thought about how funny it was that she, who knew Max so well, could not find the present he had meant for her. Sighing at the unfairness of life, she somehow managed to squeeze into her pyjamas. There wasn't much room in the tiny bathroom. She padded back to the saloon, found her torch, switched off the gas lamps and climbed into her bunk. She didn't expect to sleep but lay in the darkness staring up at the ceiling, trying to block the thoughts racing around in her head.

She did sleep and woke much later when the boat rocked violently. Immediately she knew where she was and guessed the movement was David coming back from the pub. Footsteps sounded overhead followed by a crash and loud laughter. Clare sat up. What was happening?

'Wey!! Here goes!'

There was a second crash and the sound of something rolling across the roof. Clare leapt out of bed and reached for her torch. Her heart was thumping and her hands wobbled unsteadily as she switched on the beam. As she made for the galley doors she bumped into David who had come from the back of the boat.

'Stay there,' he commanded.

He steadied her with his hands and was gone.

'Are you all right?'

Martin appeared, dressed in pyjamas with his hair sticking up at the back.

'What's happening?'

'Dunno. Let's go see.'

Above them they heard another crash and David shouting angrily. They raced through the galley and onto the deck just in time to see two large boys leaping onto the bank and haring up the tow-path. David followed but quickly gave up the chase.

'Dumb kids!' he yelled.

The boys jeered and shouted rude words back.

David shrugged his shoulders and returned to Carnival.

'Drunk! Don't suppose they realized there was anyone on board.'

He shone his torch over the cabin roof and Clare gasped. Max's garden was ruined. Every pot destroyed. Flowers and earth strewn over the roof in a jumble of broken stems and crushed petals. For the first time since Max's death Clare found herself crying. Properly crying, not the weepy tears that leaked out whenever she thought about him, but real tears that spilled from her eyes and splashed down her cheeks. She climbed onto the roof, moving amongst the mess on hands and knees, picking up pieces of broken earthenware and trying to put them together.

'Don't cry. It looks worse than it is.'

'It's ruined. It was Max's favourite thing, his

garden, and now it's ruined.'

'We can fix it. We'll buy new pots. We'll plant new flowers.'

David took Clare's hands in his and held them tightly.

'You can choose. Tell us what he liked best. It'll be even better than before.'

'Why?' shouted Clare angrily. Why did Max have to die and leave her on her own? And why did some stupid thugs have to go and wreck the thing he loved best after boats, his garden?

'Martin, get a broom. It won't look so bad when we've swept up. Come on, Clare. You help. It'll make you feel better,' David commanded.

Clare sniffed. David was right. Carefully she began to pick up the larger pieces of pot.

'Put them there, on the deck, while I get a bin bag.'

Clare found herself alone and was grateful. She wiped her eyes on the sleeve of her pyjamas and felt a bit better. The mess wasn't as bad as it could have been. She shone her torch over the roof. Three pots completely smashed, two with large cracks and one overturned.

Carefully, Clare stepped across the cabin roof to rescue the overturned one. Broken pottery bit into her bare feet and wincing she shone the torch down to see where she was going. A flash of something caught her eye. She swung the torch round like a lighthouse beam.

There it was again. A thin stick of silver, half hidden under the broken head of a red geranium. Clare's fingers lifted it from the soil. It was more than a stick. One end was shaped with tiny teeth. Holding it in her palm, Clare brushed away the soil. It was a key. A perfectly shaped silver key. She'd never seen it before. Where had it come from? Had those boys dropped it – or had someone hidden it in a tub of flowers?

Clare felt suddenly dizzy. Was this what she was searching for? Tightly, her hand closed around the key. There was no pocket in her pyjamas. She crossed the cabin roof, bumping into Martin as she climbed down onto the deck.

55

'I've got a broom. David's getting a bin bag.'

'I'll be back in a minute.' Clare avoided Martin's eyes and sniffed. 'I need a tissue.'

CHAPTER 7

A new friend

Clare slept with the key under her pillow and the next morning she hid it in her purse. She hoped it wouldn't be too long before she could try it out in the wooden box under Max's bunk. While Clare and Martin went outside to see the damaged garden David started breakfast. It was a beautiful spring morning and already the air was heavy with the smell of pollen. It was a shock to see the devastated garden by daylight. Hardly any of the flowers were left and there were three empty spaces where once there had been pots.

'We can fix it,' said Martin. 'There's a brilliant

garden centre in Merton. We'll buy new pots and fill them with flowers. Every colour you want.'

'Thanks,' said Clare. 'Canal boats should have flowers. That's what Max always said.'

The canal was getting busier. After breakfast they passed a couple of other narrow boats, both with noisy families aboard.

'It's Good Friday tomorrow,' said David. 'Won't your mum miss you over Easter?'

'She won't be on her own. She's got Alan.'

Clare felt better for remembering that. Mum would be worried about her but after the first shock she might like the freedom of not having her around. Alan certainly would.

'We get to Merton on Easter Sunday. How are you getting home? Will your mum pick you up?'

Clare hadn't given it a thought. Mum could drive but they couldn't afford a car. Did buses run over Easter? What would Mum say when Clare phoned her from Merton? She might be furious and refuse to come and get her. She might tell David and Martin that Clare had run away. It would be so embarrassing. Perhaps she should say she was meeting her mother somewhere and phone her after she'd left David and Martin. That would be better if she could get away with it.

To avoid answering the question Clare said, 'We're coming up to Cartbridge Lock. Can I work the sluice gates?'

They had to wait to use the lock. Clare moored the boat behind two narrow boats, then went ashore for a closer look at them. Max always took an interest in other narrow boats. He liked to know the names of the boats and where they'd come from. Often he would talk with the people aboard and he made many friends.

The boats waiting to use the lock weren't very interesting. Both were owned by a company called Jackman's, who specialized in canal holidays. They were painted to look like the traditional boats, but they didn't look right.

'Jackman's Fun in the Sun, Jackman's Water Baby,' said Clare, giggling.

How Max would have hated those names! She turned away and was about to return to Carnival when she noticed a sack half hidden under a gorse bush at the side of the tow-path. The sack moved. Clare remained rooted to the spot and as she watched the sack moved again. Then it grunted.

Cautiously, she approached it. It was tied roughly at the top with a thick piece of string and it smelt awful. Clare picked up a stick and gently prodded the sacking where she'd seen the movement. The sack moved again and gave a loud indignant yap.

With trembling fingers, Clare tugged at the knotted string. At first nothing happened. It was tied tightly and the string began to fray while the knot remained firmly in place.

Then Martin arrived to see what she was doing and offered her his penknife. She cut the string with one slice and gently opened out the sacking. A black nose pushed itself into her hand and a tongue licked her. It was wet and rough. It tickled and made Clare laugh.

'It's a puppy,' she said, scooping the dog up in her hands.

'Poor thing, look at the state it's in!' said

Martin indignantly.

The puppy's fur was matted together with dirt. Clare held it at arms length, laughing as the puppy pedalled the air with its legs while craning forward to lick her face.

'What shall we do with it? We can't leave it here.'

'We'll take it with us. We can give it to the police or the RSPCA when we get home.' Martin grinned suddenly. 'Unless you want to keep it. I said you should get a dog.'

'Yes!'

Clare was surprised at the fierceness in her own voice.

'I *do* want it.'

The puppy was lovely. It would be her friend.

Someone to have fun and share secrets with. Mum had Alan. She would have this puppy.

'Will David mind having it aboard? It stinks!'

'Carnival's my boat,' said Martin. 'Besides, we can bath it. It won't smell so bad then.'

David liked dogs and he didn't mind, although he teased Clare about having another mouth to feed.

'I'll pay for the dog food,' said Clare. 'I want to.'

By this time the queue for the lock was moving, so Clare shut the puppy in the galley while they took their turn.

Once they were safely at the other side they moored up and Clare set to work cleaning the puppy. She filled the galley sink with warm water and borrowed Martin's shampoo to wash it with.

'It's a he,' said David knowledgeably. 'What are you going to call him?'

'I don't know yet.'

Clare lifted the puppy into the sink. He was too big really and he wouldn't stay in the water but tried to jump on to the tiny draining board.

Martin gave her a hand and soon they were both covered with soapy bubbles.

'He's a right wriggler! Watch out, he's off again.'

'Got you!' said Clare.

The puppy shook himself.

'Aw! Get off! You're soaking me!'

'Quick, rinse him off.'

They wrapped him in a bath towel to dry him and Clare was surprised to see that he wasn't a brown dog at all, more a tawny colour with patches of white and black.

'I don't know what kind he is. He's a mixture. There's definitely Collie in there somewhere,' said David. 'And bits of terrier.'

'Medley. That's what I'll call you,' Clare replied. 'That means mixture.'

'You'd better feed him,' said David. 'He can have the sausages in the fridge.'

Clare took two sausages, cut them into pieces and put them on a saucer. At once, Medley wolfed them down and barked for more.

'He's starving,' said David. 'He needs puppy food. Are there shops near here, Clare?'

'Steep's the nearest, that's where we were yesterday.'

Clare buried her nose in Medley's damp fur. This was going to be awkward. She needed things for her dog but she couldn't risk going in to town again. Someone might recognize her.

'That's a nuisance,' said David. 'It'll make us late if we have to go that far.'

He drummed his fingers on the table and then said briskly, 'I'll go on my own this time. It'll be much quicker and someone ought to stay with Medley. Puppies chew things when they're left alone.'

Clare hoped her relief didn't show when she said, 'Thanks. And I'll give you some money because Medley is going to be my dog.'

'We'll sort that out later. Just write a list of the things you need,' said David.

When it came down to it Clare wasn't very sure what she needed. Food, of course, but what did puppies eat?

'Tinned stuff and biscuit mix,' suggested Martin. 'And you'll need two bowls. One for food and one for water.'

'A collar,' said David. 'And a lead so we can tie him up. We don't want him falling overboard the next time we go through a lock.'

'Something to chew. A squeaky toy or a rubber bone. And a bed.'

'A bed will cost a lot,' said David. 'A cardboard box will do for now.'

The only thing Clare could think of was doggie chocolate drops, so she added them to the list before handing it to David.

'You two can make some sandwiches while I'm away. We won't stop for lunch. We need to make up some time,' he said.

He tucked the list in the back pocket of his jeans and set out for Steep at a jog.

Clare and Martin busied themselves making the sandwiches and when they were finished, they played with Medley.

'This is the best holiday I've ever had,' said Martin shyly. 'We're going to Euro Disney on Easter Monday but it won't be as good as this.'

A pulse began to throb in Clare's temple. Her mouth felt dry and her skin prickled. This was the best thing that had happened to her, too. This was her moment. She was going to do it. She would come clean and tell Martin all about Max's promise and running away. Then she'd show him the key and tell him about the box

she'd found under the bunk. They could go and open it together, instead of her having to sneak around like a thief.

She opened her mouth, but before she could say anything David stepped into the galley and dumped two carrier bags on the floor.

'I'm back,' he said. 'Where's lunch?'

CHAPTER 8

Police!

It was dusk. They'd stopped only for a snatched tea and were now travelling on the last stretch of the canal before it fed into the River Wavel. They planned to continue sailing until they joined the river and then moor up somewhere for the night.

'If we keep this speed up tomorrow and Saturday we'll easily reach our parents at midday on Sunday,' said David.

It was fun sailing in the half-light. Clare leant against the handrail, with Medley asleep at her feet, straining her eyes to see the way ahead.

Already she could see the lights where the canal joined the river and in the distance a town.

'We're going left aren't we?' asked Martin, who was sitting next to Clare, studying the map by pocket torch.

'Yep. It's not much further now. You tired?' asked David.

Martin nodded and rubbed his eyes.

'Yeah. It must be all this fresh air.'

Clare pointed ahead.

'We're nearly there. There's the river.'

As Carnival travelled steadily onwards, Clare felt sad. Would this be the last time she ever sailed on the canal? Martin had promised to stay friends and invite her over but people didn't always keep promises, did they? Once he was back at school with his own friends around him again, he might forget her. She shifted her position and accidentally kicked Medley. He woke up with a start and ran around licking everyone with a slobbery tongue.

'Get down,' said David crossly pushing him off. 'Clare, keep this dog under control. We're coming up to a tricky bit.'

'Sorry.'

Clare pulled Medley away from David and tried to make him lie down again.

'He probably needs to go to the loo. It's a while since he last went.'

'Well, he'll have to wait. I'm not stopping again until we've joined the river.'

Martin screwed his face up as if he was desperate to go to the toilet himself and Clare stifled a giggle. She hoped Medley could wait, if he had an accident now it would only make David more cross.

David stared straight ahead with his hand grasped tightly around the tiller until they had safely joined the River Wavel. Clare knew it would be harder to steer now they had left the canal. The river had a current and it was much busier. Already, there were several boats moored along the bank and David had to alter his course and sail further out. Then from behind came the sound of a motor boat. It came up fast.

Clare twisted around to look and as she did, the boat switched on a bank of blue lights. Her stomach lurched, as she remembered the ambulance that had carried Max away into the night. Then panic overtook her when a siren wailed and a loudspeaker burst noisily across the water.

'Pull over. This is the river police. Pull over to the bank at once.'

'You've never heard of me. Don't say anything!'

At once, Clare grabbed Medley and disappeared through the aft deck doors and into David and Martin's cabin.

For a second time she found herself frantically looking for somewhere to hide. Not the wardrobe this time, Medley would never stay put. She rushed into the corridor and the answer was there to meet her. The bathroom. It was perfect. It had a lock and they couldn't make her come out. With the command from the loudspeaker still ringing in her ears she carried Medley into the tiny room and bolted the door behind her.

There wasn't much space. Clare put the toilet seat down and sat on it, cradling Medley in her arms.

'Sssh,' she crooned. 'It's going to be all right. But please, don't make a sound.'

Clare's hands were trembling and her heart

raced uncomfortably. How had they found her? She was going to tell Mum where she was, but in her own time. They had nearly reached Merton and it would be too cruel to be made to leave Carnival now. Would the police be cross with her? What did they do to people who had run away? She hoped they wouldn't handcuff her and make her stay in a police cell until Mum came to pick her up. Or worse still, drive her home in a police car. The shame of it!

Carnival stopped moving and Clare could hear the ropes scraping across the deck as David, or maybe Martin, tied her up.

Then there was the familiar dipping motion as people came aboard.

'Three,' counted Clare. That was David or Martin and two policemen.

Did they really need two policemen to arrest her?

She sat, statue like, hardly daring to breathe. Her ears straining for the footsteps that would mean the boys had betrayed her. She heard nothing. Five minutes passed, then ten and no one came to get her. Gradually Clare's heartbeat slowed. The boys hadn't let her down! She knew Martin wouldn't, but she hadn't been sure about David. He was older and more responsible. He'd called her a thief and he wasn't in a very good mood this evening.

Fifteen minutes later and now Medley was growing restless. He scratched at the bathroom door and whimpered. Then he squatted down and went to the toilet.

'Poor Medley,' Clare whispered.

It wasn't his fault. She knew he needed to go. She wrapped the solid stuff in toilet paper and put it down the toilet to flush away later. There was a cloth hanging behind the toilet and Clare did her best to clear up the rest of the mess. She was so busy she didn't hear the footsteps coming along the corridor. A loud knock on the bathroom door made her jump, then she heard David's voice, low and angry.

'Clare, you can come out now. They've gone.'

She unlocked the door and faced David, the dirty cloth still in her hands.

'Pooh! What a smell!'

'Medley had an accident.'

Clare dumped the cloth in the sink, rinsed her hands and flushed the toilet.

'It wasn't his fault.'

'I'm not here to talk about Medley,' snapped David. 'You're the one with the explaining to do. Come out at once.'

Clare saw Martin standing behind David and his hurt expression was even harder to bear than David's anger. Silently she went and sat at the dining table.

'What's all this about then? Why scuttle off when the police show? What are you up to?'

'Didn't they tell you?'

Clare looked up in surprise.

'No, they didn't. It was my fault they stopped us. We were sailing without lights. It was dangerous.'

'Oh!' said Clare.

'Oh! Is that all you can say? I want a bit more than that, Clare. Who are you and what have you been up to?'

'I'm Clare Francis. Max was my friend,' Clare gulped. 'Only that's not all.'

Confessing was much easier than Clare

thought. Once the truth came rushing out, she began to feel as if she were shedding a heavy load.

'You shouldn't have lied,' said Martin, when she had finished. 'You should have told us the truth. But I expect I'd have done the same thing.'

Suddenly, he smiled and asked Clare to show him the key she'd found.

'Let's get the box now and see if it fits,' he suggested.

David, however, wouldn't hear of it.

'Your mother will be worried sick. We must phone her at once and let her know that you are all right.'

'Not tonight, please,' wheedled Clare. 'We're all tired and it's too dark to go looking for a phone box. Besides, Mum doesn't have a car. If she comes tonight she'll have to ask Alan to drive her and I couldn't bear that. He'll be so angry.'

'We have to phone your mum immediately. Have you any idea how worried she must be? She needs to know you're safe. And you've made it really awkward for me. I could get into a lot of trouble for this, you know.'

'Tomorrow morning. First thing,' pleaded Clare. 'We might not find a phone box in the dark. We might get lost. It's only for one more night.'

'No, *now*,' said David firmly. 'Put your coat back on. We're going to phone your mother.'

In the end, the only telephone box they could find was broken. Clare was very glad when David said, 'It's too dark to go any further. We'll have to wait until morning.'

She hugged Medley tightly. What luck! She needed time to think. She was too tired to face her mother tonight and she was definitely too tired to cope with Alan.

CHAPTER 9

Running away again

It was still dark and there was a sharp bite to the morning air. Clare hugged Medley tightly and he wriggled in protest.

'Sorry,' she whispered. 'Put your head back down. I can't see where we're going.'

She pushed his tawny head further inside her coat. The path alongside the river was wider than a tow-path and not as bumpy. Clare was grateful. She didn't fancy a tumble in the water because she couldn't see where she was putting her feet. She walked as quickly as she dared, wanting to put as much distance between her and Carnival before it grew light.

'Mind you,' she said softly to Medley. 'They might not come after me. They might be glad I've gone.'

Clare had had a restless night. She couldn't get comfortable and she couldn't sleep, as unwanted thoughts flitted around her head. What would Mum say? Clare could cope with her mother being angry. But what if she wasn't? What if she was pleased to have Clare out of the way? She might wish she hadn't made that television appeal. She might not want Clare home now she'd got Alan to herself. What would happen to her then?

The night wore on and Clare's eyes grew gritty with tiredness, but still she didn't sleep. Her thoughts became wilder and wilder, until her head was so scrambled it felt as if it was going to explode. That was when the idea came. She'd run away. Properly this time. Running away was simple and this time she wouldn't be on her own. She had Medley.

She lay awake then, watching the luminous hands of the alarm clock Martin had lent her. At five fifteen she'd slipped out of bed, dressed, stowed her pyjamas into her rucksack and left. That was it. Easy!

She walked briskly for the first ten minutes but Medley was getting heavier and the straps of her rucksack were beginning to bite through her anorak. Ahead, Clare could make out the outline of a bridge and as she neared it, a car drove over the top.

'A road, Medley. I wonder where it goes.'

She stopped to wriggle her rucksack into a more comfortable position.

'We've got to leave the river. Carnival will be coming this way. But where does the road go to? I wish I could remember.'

Clare thought back to the map Martin was looking at yesterday evening. There was a town marked on it, lying to the right of the river. What was it called? She closed her eyes for a moment and tried to picture it.

'Denton!'

'Are you hungry, Medley? Shall we go to Denton and get something to eat?'

Medley pushed his head out of her coat and

tried to lick Clare's nose.

'Yuk! Don't eat me! We'll go to town and I'll buy you something nicer to chew.'

As they approached the bridge the way ahead split. The main path followed the river, while a second, narrower path sloped steeply upwards towards the road. Clare plodded up it, the long grass snatching at her trainers and soaking them with dew. As she neared the top another car passed and Clare turned her face from its headlights. The car rushed by without even slowing and suddenly Clare felt very alone.

At the top she stopped to catch her breath and Medley began wriggling in earnest.

'Stop it! I'll drop you.'

She looked around her. If she was going to Denton, she would have to turn right and walk over the bridge. It was getting lighter now and further down the road was a bus shelter.

'There's a bus stop up there. It's probably got a seat inside. When we get there I'll put you on the lead. You can have a walk. I expect you need the toilet again.'

Medley continued to fidget and Clare quickened her pace.

'Here we are. You can get down now.'

The bus shelter smelt sour and uninviting. Cigarette butts littered the floor and a couple of empty cans clanged noisily against the toe of Clare's trainers. Heaped on one end of the bench was a bundle of rags and old newspapers. Clare made for the other end and sat down.

'Pooh!'

The stink inside was awful. Clare's nose twitched in disgust. She slipped her arms out of her rucksack and quickly began rummaging inside for Medley's lead.

'We won't stay here long!'

She sensed the movement a split second before her eyes saw it. Her heart beat quickened and she grabbed Medley by the scruff of his neck. At the other end of the bench the pile of rags and newspapers began to scatter.

Clare stifled the scream rising inside her and stared in horror at the writhing pile of rubbish. Newspapers fell away revealing first a matted beard and then a head covered with straggly grey hair. Hands next, old and gnarled, poking out from a coat tied with string. The smell grew stronger and Clare had to breathe through her mouth to stop herself from gagging.

'Spare any change, miss?'

The voice was hoarse and the request ended with a hacking cough.

'Spare me somethin' for a cuppa tea.'

Immediately Clare tightened the neck of her rucksack and scooped a surprised Medley off the floor.

'No, sorry. I–I–'

Clare fled the bus shelter and stumbled along the road in the direction of Denton. When she was sure the tramp hadn't followed her, she stopped to lean against a telegraph pole. She was still trembling with shock. He was probably just a poor old tramp, she told herself shakily. He didn't mean any harm. She had been completely terrified but she didn't want to admit it, even to herself.

She dumped Medley back on the ground and found his lead. The sky was much lighter but when she looked at her watch to check the time, Clare realized she'd forgotten to put it on. She'd left it on Carnival, lying with the other odds and ends in the small wicker basket Max kept in the galley.

Both the thought of Max and the tramp made Clare feel very sad and lonely. Wherever was she going? She had no idea. Running away wouldn't solve anything. She'd run away once and it had caused more problems, yet here she was, running for a second time. She couldn't carry on like this or she'd end up like that tramp; alone and with nowhere to go. Besides, if she ran away now she would never get another chance to find the present that Max had left her. To run away again would be to betray Max.

Tears welled up in her eyes and impatiently Clare brushed them away.

'What shall I do?' she asked herself.

Deep in her heart Clare knew there was only one answer. She would have to go back to Carnival and face everyone. She would go with David to find a phone box and let Mum know she was safe. Mum might be  furious but she wouldn't leave her. What ever made her think she would! Anyway, Alan wouldn't stand for that. He'd take control and be heavy handed and cross. He'd like that! Clare giggled at the thought.

'I bet he keeps me in,' she told Medley. 'He'll make me stay in my room and only let me out for meals and school.'

Once she'd made up her mind to go back, Clare was keen to get on with it. With a sinking heart she realized she'd have to pass the bus stop again, but she would walk behind it this time. Maybe, the tramp wouldn't see her. Clare put her rucksack back on her back and pulled Medley away from the telegraph pole. He was indignant, not wanting to leave the lovely doggy smells around it.

'Come on you. I'll carry you if you don't walk sensibly.'

Reluctantly Medley turned away and followed Clare back along the road. It was growing steadily lighter and a few more cars passed them. Clare increased her pace as a new and frightening thought came to her. What if Carnival had left already? David was keen to make an early start to make up for lost time.

Panic made her jog. The rucksack bounced uncomfortably on her back as she trotted down the road. Medley thought it was a game and gambolled beside her, ears pricked and tongue lolling. They ran behind the bus shelter and on towards the bridge.

'Come on, Medley, come on!'

They slid down the slope from the bridge to the river, stopping at the edge of the water for Clare to catch her breath.

'Which way, Medley?'

Should they go on to the mooring place where Clare had left Carnival, or would the boys have already sailed?

In the end it was Medley who made the decision. There was a swan gliding along the water and he chased off in the direction from which she'd come earlier that morning.

'Come back, you daft dog.'

Clare yanked the lead and then ran with him, anxious now to return to her friends.

Carnival was still at her mooring and the spring sunshine on her paintwork made the old boat sparkle with life. A lump rose in Clare's throat. Carnival. Hers and Max's. She was more than a boat. She was a friend too. Clare was glad she'd come back. And there was another friend, for suddenly Clare noticed David sitting on the cabin roof. He hadn't seen her for he was reading a book. Clare watched him for a moment and then cleared her throat.

'Hello.'

Carefully David marked his place with a piece of card then laid the book down in his lap.

He didn't answer but looked at her gravely.

'I . . .'

Clare was about to say she'd been for an early morning walk with Medley, but what was the point? It was better to come clean and be honest for once.

'I was going to run away,' she said boldly.

'I know.'

'Are you cross?'

David thought for a moment.

'Running away is easy. You came back. That takes courage.'

Clare felt her face go hot and she stared at the toe of her shoe.

'Where's Martin?'

'Asleep. I was just going to wake him. Do you want to do it?'

Clare nodded and lifting Medley from beside her she climbed aboard.

'Clare . . .'

David's eyes were soft.

'Don't go that way. Come over the roof and leave your bag in the saloon. We won't bother to tell Martin about this morning.'

CHAPTER 10

Confessions

David wanted to start the telephone call to Clare's mum but Clare knew this was something she had to do herself and she begged David to let her. In the end, David agreed but he waited outside the telephone kiosk so he could speak to Mrs Francis as well. Martin was nearby, playing with Medley, and Clare found she was glad she could see them both while she dialled home.

The phone did not ring for long and when someone picked up the receiver Clare panicked and only just stopped herself from slamming down her end.

'Loxford 397859. Hello?'

It was Mum, not Alan, and after her first stuttering hello Clare found words came easily to her. There were lots of tears – Mum cried too – but no cross words.

'I might be cross later,' Mum laughed, 'when the relief of finding you has worn off, but for now I'm just so pleased to hear your voice.'

Mrs Francis wanted to speak to David and after a bit, Clare heard David ask if she could finish the trip to Merton with them.

'She's a great sailor,' Clare heard him say.

Mrs Francis was non-committal.

'She might let you,' David reported. 'She wants to see you first. The police want to see you too. Besides, you both need to talk. Running away is a big thing.'

Mrs Francis promised to come at once and although Clare was still worried, it was a happier party that returned to Carnival to wait for her.

'Breakfast,' said David, heading straight for the galley.

He cooked a mountain of bacon sandwiches, which they ate with brown sauce, and huge mugs of tea. Clare's appetite had returned now there were no secrets to hide and she ate heartily, throwing scraps of bacon to Medley.

With breakfast cleared away, Clare suggested they did some cleaning. Over the years, Max had collected a number of brass trinkets to decorate

Carnival in true narrow boat style. There was a small kettle, a warming pan, several ornaments and a few horse brasses. Today Clare took down the horse brasses from the saloon wall, and brought everything up onto Carnival's roof to polish in the glorious spring sunshine.

'You want *me* to dust!' David exclaimed in mock horror.

But soon he was polishing a horse brass whilst telling funny stories of when he was at school. He was in the middle of a tale about the PE teacher when Clare saw her mother. The laughter died on her lips and her face froze.

'Not funny enough?' said David. 'Well, how about this?'

Martin nudged him in the ribs and nodded towards the bank where a pretty woman and a plump, balding man were carefully picking their way along the river path towards Carnival. Behind them was a policewoman.

'Is that your mum?'

Clare nodded and she answered hoarsely, 'She's brought Alan with her and the police!'

At once David laid down the horse brass he

was cleaning.

'Your mum doesn't have a car. How else could she get here? Anyway, she was probably glad of Alan's company. You gave her a huge shock running away like that. And you knew you'd have to see the police, so why not straight away? It gets it over and done with.' He paused and said in a more conspiratorial tone, 'Don't worry about Alan. Leave him to me.'

Clare's body felt like wood as she climbed down from the cabin roof and stood waiting for her mother to reach the boat. She was aware of Martin hurriedly putting the cleaning things back in the saloon, but before he'd finished her mother arrived. She stood uncertainly at the water's edge and for the life of her, Clare couldn't think of one thing to say.

She was grateful for David who immediately took control. He welcomed Mrs Francis and the policewoman aboard, showing them into the saloon, before whisking Martin and Alan away for a walk.

'Oh, Clare,' said Mrs Francis wrapping her arms around her daughter and Clare found herself hugging her mother back.

After the policewoman had left, Mrs Francis and Clare talked for a long time. Clare told her mother everything, from how she felt about Max dying to how she loathed Alan. To her surprise, Mum talked too. Telling Clare how lonely she'd been when Dad left and how she needed someone to be there for her.

'You've got me,' said Clare accusingly.

'Of course I have, but you are still a child. I need someone my own age.'

'Why Alan though? You're far too good for him!' squeaked Clare. 'He's old and fat and he's losing his hair.'

'Alan's only five years older than me,' said

Mrs Francis. 'And how many times have I told you that looks aren't everything? Alan can't stop his hair falling out. It's what's inside that counts. Alan is kind and generous.'

'He's a bully. He hates me having fun. He stops you from letting me do things.'

'Alan isn't a bully. He cares about you very much but he doesn't know how to handle you. He hasn't got any children of his own, remember, and you don't give him a chance. You're rude and angry when he's around. He may seem gruff, but he's only trying to protect me.'

Clare's face flamed. It was true. Alan did bring out the worst in her.

'I don't want to share you,' she mumbled sheepishly. 'Alan gets in the way.'

Mrs Francis took Clare's hand in both of her own.

'Love, I know what you're thinking but it won't happen. I'll never stop loving you and I'll never leave either. You're my daughter! You mean more to me than the world. I'll always be here for you. I promise you that. Only you won't

be a child for ever. One day you'll leave home
yourself. Just think how lonely I'll be then if I
don't have any of my own friends. You have to
share me, Clare. It's not fair to expect anything
else.'

Clare fell silent. She hadn't thought about it
like that. All she could see was Alan swooping
into her life and carrying her mother away,
without her.

'Please try and give Alan a chance. Once you
get to know him properly I'm sure you'll like
him. He's very fond of you.'

'Will you tell him to stop bossing me about?'

'Will you stop being surly and rude?'

'I'll try.'

'Then I think you'll find Alan is less bossy. He doesn't know what to do with you when you're so mean the whole time. Give him a chance and you might surprise yourself. Trust me, he's a very kind man.'

'It's not going to be easy but I'll try.'

'Thank you,' said Mrs Francis.

Suddenly another thought struck Clare.

'What about Medley? I bet Alan won't let me keep him.'

'Clare!' sighed Mrs Francis, giving her daughter an affectionate shake. 'There you go again. Alan is not an ogre! Anyway, keeping Medley is nothing to do with him. It's my house and I'm the one you need to ask.'

'Can I, Mum? Please can I keep him?'

Mrs Francis laughed.

'I think it's a very good idea. You'll have someone of your own to look after. Who knows, Medley might even help you to see how much I do for you!'

'And can I stay on Carnival until we reach Merton?'

Clare dug her fingernails into the palms of her hands and willed her mother to say yes.

'Are you sure David and Martin want you to stay?'

'I think so.'

'If David and Martin say yes *and* if Alan agrees to drive me over to Merton on Sunday to pick you up, then I don't see why not.'

Clare threw herself at her mother.

'Get off, you great daftie. You're squashing me! Alan hasn't agreed yet. He might have better things to do than chase around the countryside after a runaway twelve-year-old!'

When they went to look for Alan and the boys they found them feeding a family of swans gathered around Carnival. The cygnets were cute and fluffy and it was difficult to imagine them going through the awkward, ugly stage before they grew into swans. Mum was right, thought Clare suddenly, you couldn't help the way you looked but you could do something about the way you acted. She would try to be nice to Alan and maybe, and it was a big maybe, in time she would get to like him.

'OK?' asked Martin, pulling Clare to one side.

'OK.'

'Are you allowed to stay until we reach Merton?'

'Yes. Well, that is . . .' Clare drew breath and for the first time ever managed to look at Alan when she spoke to him. 'Mum says I can stay, if you'll come to pick me up on Sunday. Please.'

'Of course I will,' said Alan.

'Thanks.'

'Great!' cheered Martin.

He gave Clare a meaningful look and her heart missed a beat as she remembered the small key, now hanging in the galley, waiting to be tried in the mysterious wooden box.

'I expect you're keen to get going,' said Mrs Francis hesitantly. 'But would you like to go out for something to eat? It would be my treat.'

'Great,' said David. 'I'm fed up with cooking.'

CHAPTER 11

Opening the box

Mrs Francis and Alan left for home straight after lunch. Clare stood in the car park, waving until Alan's car was no more than a blue speck in the distance.

'Come on,' said David finally. 'We've got to go.'

He walked briskly. Clare and Martin hurried behind, competing with each other to see who could tell the silliest jokes. And soon Clare had that light-headed feeling you get walking home from school on the last day of term.

'Can we open the box when we get back?'

asked Martin, when David paused to let them catch up. 'Before we leave?'

'Definitely not,' answered David, but there was a twinkle in his eye.

'It might not be the right key.'

Clare sounded casual but her heart hammered painfully inside her chest. When you wanted something desperately it often didn't happen. It was better to pretend it didn't matter.

'We can always bust the lock,' said Martin cheerfully.

Clare was shocked. Max would never have broken something just to get into it.

'It's not that important. If it isn't the right key let's leave it. Max must have left the key somewhere.'

David snorted.

'Not that important! Who are you trying to kid? Don't worry, if there's any lock busting to do, then I'll pick the lock.'

'*You* pick a lock! We'll still be here at Christmas,' said Martin. 'Anyway, it *is* the right key. I have this feeling.'

'Good,' said Clare lightly. 'I'm allowed to stay

until Easter Sunday. I don't think I could wait until Christmas!'

The box was large and rectangular in shape with the initials M.D.J.P. painted on the side. Carefully David laid it on the saloon table.

'Maximillian David James Parry,' said David. 'I was named after him. I'm David James Parry.'

'You open it,' said Martin to Clare.

Now that the moment had come Clare felt suddenly shy. She would have much rather opened the box on her own. As if sensing the atmosphere even Medley was silent as she put the tiny key into the lock. It glided in, turning

smoothly and allowing the lock to snap open at once.

'Oh!'

Clare had steeled herself for disappointment and the ease at which the box opened was almost an anticlimax.

'What's inside?'

Martin squinted over her shoulder as she gently raised the lid. The box was half-full with a piece of tissue paper covering its contents. It crackled and folded itself around her hands when Clare lifted it up to lay it on the table. Underneath was a large brown envelope, fastened with an elastic band. Clare laid it on the table next to the paper.

'Go on, open it.'

'But it's your boat. This is yours, too.'

'Go on, open it. There might be something in it for you.'

With shaking fingers, Clare removed the elastic band and tipped the contents of the envelope onto the table. It was mostly receipts, pieces of paper with details of all the purchases made to restore Carnival. Impatiently Clare sorted through them, but planks of wood, claw hammers and tins of paint were of no interest to her.

'What's that?'

Martin's fingers seized upon a scrap of paper with a number on.

'Is this a clue? The number to a safe or something?'

'Carnival doesn't have a safe,' said Clare, studying the piece of paper. 'That looks like a telephone number. It's the Loxford code.'

'We could try ringing it.'

'It's probably the number of the local hardware shop,' said Clare.

She pushed a stray strand of hair behind her ears.

'There's nothing here for me.'

'What else is in the box?'

David stretched over and took out a second bundle.

'Photographs. A record of how Max restored Carnival. Hey! These are really interesting. Have you seen them before, Clare?'

'Yes, I have. Max kept meaning to get an album for them. They're all dated on the back. He was going to write little captions to go under each photograph.'

'We can still do that,' said Martin, excitedly. 'We could stick the receipts in too. Then Carnival will have her own log.'

'Who's this, Clare? Do you know this woman?'

David handed Clare a photograph. It wasn't like the others. It was smaller and thicker and the brown and white image was faded. She stared at it for a while before passing it on to Martin.

'I don't know. She's beautiful isn't she?'

The woman in the picture was young with dark hair coiled around her head in an elegant way. She wore old-fashioned clothes and a brooch similar to the one Clare's Nan wore when she was alive.

'There's nothing written on the back.'

Martin handed the photograph back to Clare.

'His girlfriend maybe?'

'Maybe.'

Suddenly, fiercely, Clare hoped that it was. Max had never spoken of his private life but it was nice to think that he had loved someone once.

'Is this another sweetheart, perhaps?!'

Martin held up a photograph and grinned mischievously.

'Rubbish!'

Clare snatched the picture from him and laid

it face down on the table. It was the same one her mother had given to the television when she was missing. Taken at school last year, there had been four little ones and one big one in the pack. Clare remembered sending Max the photo in his Christmas card. The thought that he'd hidden it away with his other treasures made her eyes smart. Briskly she reached for the box and removed another piece of tissue paper. Underneath lay a slim, velvet pouch. Carefully she laid it on the table.

'What is it?' asked Martin eagerly.

Clare smiled. She'd forgotten Max had this. It was something he'd used a lot once but recently there'd been other things to fill their time.

'Mouth organ,' she said.

She slid the mouth organ into the palm of her hand and turned it so that Martin could see.

'It's silver and it has his name engraved on it. It's very old. His father gave it to him for his eighteenth birthday. He used to play for me. He taught me lots of songs.'

'Is that it? Is that the thing Max wanted you to have?'

'No.'

Clare was sure it wasn't. Max would have told her if it was the mouth organ. She put it back inside its pouch and turned once more to the box.

There wasn't much else in it. An old pipe, not Max's for he didn't smoke, and a rather special Swiss army knife.

'That's it.' Try as she did she couldn't hide the disappointment in her voice.

'Are you sure there's nothing in here meant for you?'

Martin fingered the objects arranged on the table.

'Maybe he meant you to have the knife.'

'He said something special. He said I'd *know*. Whatever he was thinking of, it isn't here.'

'We'll search the boat then,' said Martin. 'Tonight when we moor up. You haven't searched properly because we interrupted you. We're bound to find it.'

'Thanks,' said Clare.

Hastily she began to stow Max's things back into his box. Think of something else, she scolded herself. Think of the fun you've had on this trip. She concentrated on other things and it worked. By the time everything was put away, the pain had nearly gone.

They sailed late into the evening, for David and Martin's parents were expecting them on Sunday and there was still a way to go. It was fun sailing on the river, but Clare missed the quietness of the canal. The river was full of people and bustle while the canal felt more peaceful. Max would have understood how she felt. She hugged Medley close to her and he wriggled sideways to lick her nose.

Clare wished they could sail on forever. She dreaded stopping for the night. She didn't want to search Carnival for Max's present. Could it be because he'd already given her so much more? New friends, a fresh start with her mother and a dog of her very own? Or was it because she was afraid that there was nothing else to find? Clare remembered Mum's words when she first told her of Max's promise. 'Old people say things they don't mean. They get confused.'

Max was old but never confused. Or had he been? He was having a heart attack, after all. Perhaps he hadn't known what he was saying. It wasn't a comforting thought. When David asked if everyone could manage to keep going for another half-hour she readily agreed.

'Yes, keep going,' she answered. 'I could sail all night!'

CHAPTER 12

Something from Max

The following day it rained. When it was her turn at the helm, Clare sat hunched in her anorak, one hand tucked under her arm for warmth, blinking away the raindrops falling from her hood and fringe. Medley refused to join her, preferring the warmth and fug of the saloon where David was revising and Martin reading a thriller.

It suited Clare to be alone. So much had happened since Max's funeral she could hardly believe that less than a week had passed. She missed him terribly. There were hundreds of things she wanted to tell him. Lots of questions she wanted to ask.

The night before they had made a thorough search of Carnival, but the old boat had no secrets to share. There were no hidden cupboards or mysterious boxes holding a special present for Clare. The longer they searched the quieter Clare became. What would the boys think of her? All that chaos she had caused in her search for something that didn't exist. Pity was the feeling she feared the most. She couldn't bear to be pitied. So when Martin made the offer, she was sharper than she meant to be.

Hating herself for the way his face crumpled at her coldness.

'I'd like you to have something from Carnival. Anything you want. An ornament, a picture, the mouth organ. Something for you to remember Max by.'

'No thanks.'

'But you must. Max wanted you to.'

'How do you know what Max wanted? He didn't leave me anything. It wouldn't be the same if I took something.'

'I'll choose for you then.'

'No!'

'Leave it, Martin,' said David gently.

Clare shot him a grateful look and in a kinder voice she said to Martin, 'I've had something already. Two new friends and my own dog. I couldn't forget Max now if I tried.'

After sailing all day Saturday there was only a little of their journey left. They tied up a few miles from Merton. On Sunday morning, Easter Sunday, David made an enormous breakfast of egg, bacon, sausage, grilled tomatoes, mushrooms and fried bread. Then he surprised

Martin and Clare by giving them both a chocolate Easter egg. Clare was feeling quite cheerful now. It was impossible to stay miserable with David and Martin for too long.

'I'll clear up,' she offered after breakfast.

'I'll help,' said Martin. 'We'll have to tidy the boat as well. Can't let Mum think we've been living in a pig sty.'

Clare was nervous about meeting Martin's parents, even though they knew about her running away; David had phoned them to tell them all about it. So she set to work cleaning Carnival as hard as she could. At least they would have no complaints about that!

Tidying up the tiny cabin, Clare remembered trying to hide in the wardrobe from David and Martin. Max would have loved that! He had a terrific sense of humour. Suddenly Clare

118

grinned. It would have been nice to have a present from him, something he'd chosen especially for her. But she didn't need it. Max had been a good friend and there were many special memories of the times shared together. It was enough.

Her cheerfulness lasted until they reached Merton and David called them up onto the deck.

'We're here and so are Mum and Dad.'

Clare felt momentarily sick and would have loitered in the galley had not Martin taken her hand and dragged her through the boat and onto the aft deck with him. Shyly Clare stood next to David, her fingers itching to take over the tiller as he smartly brought Carnival to a halt alongside her new mooring. There was nothing for her to do however. David was in control, throwing the mooring rope to a tall man with the same dark, curly hair as himself. The boat lurched as the man and a woman with a warm smile clambered aboard and engulfed everyone with hugs.

'And you must be Clare. We've heard lots about you. It's nice to meet you at last.'

Clare smiled shyly.

Mrs Parry let her go and led everyone back towards the galley.

'I've brought some cakes. I expect you're all starving, as usual.'

When she reached the saloon step Medley launched himself on her like a missile. Wagging his tail he jumped about, his tongue licking every bit of her it could reach.

'Down boy,' said Clare. 'Down.'

'It's all right dear. My, what a friendly little puppy!'

Medley gave Mrs Parry one last, huge lick and then set about introducing himself to Mr Parry.

'Whoa there, steady boy.'

Mr Parry pushed Medley down and at once he began careering about the boat, growling and worrying the legs of the table. Suddenly he quietened and before Clare realized what was happening, he crouched in the corner of the room and began to wee.

'No! Medley, stop! Outside now.'

Frantically Clare tugged at his collar, but it was too late. Medley rolled his eyes in relief, straightened up and scratched the floor with his hind legs. Comfortable now he took himself off to his cardboard box and curled up inside.

'Sorry,' said Clare.

'Don't worry,' said Martin. 'Blot it with this.'

'Better pull the carpet up,' said Mrs Parry. 'If that seeps into the floorboards you'll never get rid of the smell.'

'Here, let me.'

Martin squatted down besides Clare and began to lift the carpet. Underneath was a layer of yellowing newspaper and Martin peeled back the sheets that were damp.

'That was lucky. It's soaked up the . . .'

His voice trailed away and Clare looked at

him sharply.

'What is it?'

'A safe,' said Martin. 'A floor safe. You said Carnival didn't have one!'

In one hand he held a piece of soggy newspaper and with the other he pointed to a metal square with a flat dial set into the floorboards.

'It's a combination,' said Mr Parry, coming over to have a look. 'You need to know the number before you can open it.'

Martin rose and without a word disappeared into the cabin. Moments later he returned, triumphantly waving a scrap of paper.

'The number in the wooden chest!'

He sat on the floor and began to twiddle the dial, first clockwise then anticlockwise and every now and then there was a small click.

'Where did you learn to open a safe?' asked Mrs Parry in astonishment.

'Ssh!'

Martin silenced her with a wave of his hand.

'It's not right. Too many numbers. The number on the paper has eleven but I think we only need six of them.'

'Try leaving out the first five,' suggested Clare. '01432 is definitely the code for Loxford. Max could have written that down to fool people. He was very smart.'

Martin tried again and Clare noticed that his hand trembled slightly as he twisted the dial.

'That's not it either. The door won't budge.'

'Try the last six numbers backwards,' said David.

Martin tried and when he looked up again his green eyes sparkled with excitement.

'Cracked it!'

Everyone crowded forward as he pulled the

door open to reveal a small, square safe set in the floorboards.

'Personal documents,' said Martin lifting an old passport, driving licence and birth certificate out of the safe.

'Yours now,' remarked Mr Parry, taking them from Martin and laying them on the table.

Under the documents was an old ivory jewellery box. Carefully, Martin lifted it out.

'You open it,' he said to Clare.

'No.'

Clare could hardly speak. Her heart was banging ferociously and her hands shaking.

Martin carried the jewellery box to the table to open it. Inside, nestled against the faded green velvet lining, were a silver locket and a cameo brooch.

'That was Max's mother's,' said Mr Parry nudging the brooch with his finger.

'Is this hers too?'

Martin laid the locket in the palm of his hand to open it. Inside were two photographs. A man on one side, a woman on the other.

'Yes, that was hers too. The pictures are of

herself and her husband. They were taken just after they got married.'

'It says something on the back. *"To my dearest Eliza with all my love Stanley."'*

'That's right. Eliza and Stanley. I suppose these things all belong to you now, Martin. You are a lucky boy,' said Mr Parry.

'There's something else.'

Martin went back to the safe and pulled out a long package wrapped in thick purple tissue paper. Clare's mouth went dry. It was her favourite colour and Max knew that. Whenever he gave her presents he always chose purple wrapping paper.

Silently she watched as Martin began to peel back the layers. He only got so far before his eyes widened and he hastily fastened the paper again. Smiling at Clare he handed her the package.

She took it, her hand reaching out in slow motion as if in a dream. The layers of tissue paper fell away and Clare went to sit at the table so as not to drop any of them. If this was from Max she wanted to keep all of it. Paper too!

Inside the package was a boat carved from

wood. Clare recognized it immediately. It was a model of Carnival, identical in every detail, right down to the roses and castles paint work. She held it up for everyone to see and as she did, the name on its side caught her eye. The boat was Carnival – only something was different. So this was the gift she was meant to have! Lady Clare, carved by Max in memory of the good times they'd shared together on Carnival.

'I knew he wouldn't let you down,' said Martin smugly.

Clare couldn't answer. A lump the size of a golf ball was working its way down her throat. Max was as good as his word. How could she have doubted him?

126

'You'll still come and sail Carnival? Now you've got your own boat?' asked Martin.

The golf ball had gone. Suddenly Clare felt very light-headed.

'Of course I will,' she said, beaming. 'Try stopping me!'

About the Author

I live in Hampshire, on a fish farm, with my husband, our three small children and 300,000 rainbow trout. I used to work as a laboratory technician and then a teacher before I started to write full time.

I live within walking distance of a canal and I often walk along it. There's always so much to see which helps me to think up ideas for stories. The idea for *Carnival* came from watching the canal boats and thinking that it would be fun to live on one for a while.

When I'm not writing I like reading, swimming, aerobics, animals and helping to feed the fish!